Watch Your Tongue,
CECILY
BEASLEY

written by Lane Fredrickson

illustrated by Jon Davis

STERLING CHILDREN'S BOOKS
New York

For Tigger and Sissy, my own little worm eaters.—LF

For Laura and Greta.—JD

STERLING CHILDREN'S BOOKS
New York
An Imprint of Sterling Publishing
387 Park Avenue South
New York, NY 10016

STERLING CHILDREN'S BOOKS and the distinctive Sterling Children's Books logo are trademarks of Sterling Publishing Co., Inc.

© 2012 by Lane Fredrickson
Illustrations © 2012 by Jon Davis

Designed by Katrina Damkoehler.

ISBN 978-1-4027-7089-0 (hardcover)

Library of Congress Cataloging-in-Publication Data Available

Distributed in Canada by Sterling Publishing
c/o Canadian Manda Group, 165 Dufferin Street
Toronto, Ontario, Canada M6K 3H6
Distributed in the United Kingdom by GMC Distribution Services
Castle Place, 166 High Street, Lewes, East Sussex, England BN7 1XU
Distributed in Australia by Capricorn Link (Australia) Pty. Ltd.
P.O. Box 704, Windsor, NSW 2756, Australia

For information about custom editions, special sales, and premium and corporate purchases, please contact Sterling Special Sales at 800-805-5489 or specialsales@sterlingpublishing.com.

Manufactured in China
Lot #:
2 4 6 8 10 9 7 5 3 1
03/12

www.sterlingpublishing.com/kids

Cecily Beasley was never polite.

She never said, "Thank you,"

or "Please,"

or "Good night."

She tap-danced on tables.

She cartwheeled in dirt.

And she wrote, "I won't share" on the front of her shirt.

She sucked up spaghetti in one giant slurp.

ARRP

And she'd laugh if she belched out a loud, stinky burp.

But those aren't the worst things that Cecily did.
That mannerless, cartwheeling, toy-hogging kid
would stick out her tongue, put her thumbs in her ears,
and make dreadful faces at teachers and peers.

A boy named Bernard said, "You know, that's bad luck.
If you do it too much, then your tongue might get stuck."

When Bernard had a birthday, the cake was in place,
and Cecily sang with a smirk on her face.
Then just when the very last note had been sung,
something horrible happened to Cecily's tongue.

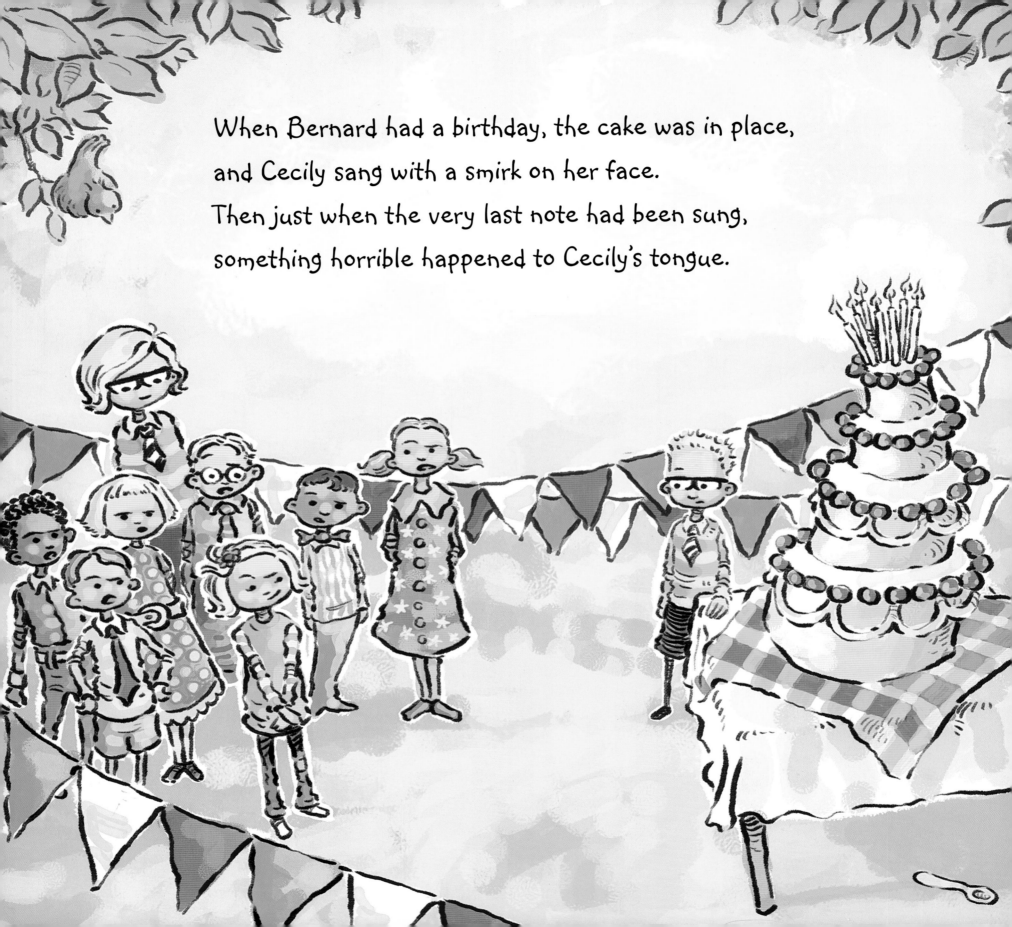

She stuck her tongue out

and it stayed there—it froze.

She screamed when she noticed her mouth wouldn't close.

A bird hovered near her and happily cooed,
dropping twig after twig on her tongue as she shooed.

She ran home to her parents and yelled, "It's a bird!"
But a gruff, muffled gurgle was all that they heard.
By then, on her tongue, a whole nest had been made,
and the bird sat content on the eggs it had laid.

They drove to the doctor as fast as they could.

He checked out her tongue and he said, "It's not good. . . .

It's a Mockingbeak Tongue-snatcher, rude and tenacious.

They roost on the tongues of the loud and audacious.

They tend to get feisty. Don't mess with that nest.

No, patiently waiting is what I suggest.

You'll be fine, but no cartwheels 'til ALL the eggs hatch.

There are surely more serious things one could catch."

That bird scratched up Cecily's tongue with its toes.

It chirped, and its feathers got stuck in her nose.

So she stayed in her bedroom
for thirteen days straight.

'Til she finally went nuts
from the bird-sitting wait.

She went out for a walk and she heard someone shouting,

Some children were scoffing and stopping to linger.
They were joking and laughing and pointing a finger.

Well, Cecily desperately wanted to scream,
to stomp and make faces, and let off some steam.
But toting this bird and its young on her tongue,
the insults she'd normally sling went unslung.

peep!

And then a chick hatched! It was out of its shell!
Poor Cecily sighed, thinking all would be well.
The chick raised its head and the people could see
it was looking at Cecily, cute as can be.

Then it opened its mouth like it wanted to speak,

and it stuck out its tongue
from its little bird beak!

Then things started happening frightfully fast.
The rest of the eggs began hatching at last.
As Cecily watched, one by one, they were sprung.
Each hatchling looked up, and it stuck out its tongue.

Why, these rude little Tongue-snatchers! Cecily thought.
They ought to have manners. They ought to be taught.

She thought about kindness and rudeness, and then
she suddenly saw just how awful she'd been.
It wasn't so funny, it wasn't so fun,
when somebody else was the tongue-sticking one.

Cecily went home and she worked on a letter
that would make both Bernard and herself feel much better.
Her heart felt so happy and snappy and good.
She planned to be nicer whenever she could.

When—at last!—all those
tongue-snatching vagrants took flight,
Cecily found that her tongue was all right.

POP

peep!

Just once, she was tempted to make a mean face.
But she struggled and squeezed out a smile in its place.
Though she wasn't quite certain, she thought she had heard
the sound of a Mockingbeak tongue-snatching bird.

Now Cecily Beasley is much more polite.

She always says, "Thank you,"

and "Please,"

and "Good night."